Rub-a-dub-dub: Three Men and a Pancake

Written by Katie Dale

Illustrated by Steve Stone

Crabtree Publishing Company

www.crabtreebooks.com

Crabtree Publishing Company
www.crabtreebooks.com
1-800-387-7650

PMB 59051,
350 Fifth Ave., 59th Floor
New York, NY 10118

616 Welland Ave.
St. Catharines, ON
L2M 5V6

Published by Crabtree Publishing in 2016

Series editor: Melanie Palmer
Series designer: Peter Scoulding
Cover designer: Cathryn Gilbert
Series advisor: Catherine Glavina
Editor: Petrice Custance
Notes to adults: Reagan Miller
Prepress technician: Ken Wright
Print production coordinator: Margaret Amy Salter

Text © Katie Dale 2015
Illustration © Steve Stone 2015

Printed in Canada/012016/BF20151123

First published in
2015 by Franklin Watts
(A division of Hachette
Children's Books)

Library and Archives Canada
Cataloguing in Publication

Dale, Katie, author
    Rub-a-dub-dub : three men and a pancake /
Katie Dale ; illustrated by Steve Stone.

(Tadpoles fairytale twists)
Issued in print and electronic formats.
ISBN 978-0-7787-2463-6 (bound).--
ISBN 978-0-7787-2566-4 (paperback).--
ISBN 978-1-4271-7722-3 (html)

    I. Stone, Steve, 1974-, illustrator II. Title. III.
Series: Tadpoles. Fairytale twists

PZ7.D157Ru 2016   j823'.92   C2015-907113-5
                                       C2015-907114-3

Library of Congress
Cataloging-in-Publication Data

CIP available at Library of Congress

This story is based on the traditional fairy tale,
The Big Pancake, but with a new twist.
Can you make up your own twist for the story?

Once upon a Tuesday, a baker
decided to cook his biggest
and best pancake ever.
It was ENORMOUS!

He tossed it once, and then twice, and then—WHOOPS!—the pancake flew right out the kitchen window!

"I'm free!" cried the pancake happily, rolling down the hill.

"Come back!" cried the baker, chasing after him.

"No way!" called the pancake, whirling down the hill. "I'm on a roll!"

"Come back!" cried the butcher,
joining the chase.

"No way!" cried the pancake,
whizzing down the hill. "Watch
me fly!"

"Come back!" cried the candlestick maker, running after them all.

"No way!" cried the pancake.

But suddenly he stopped rolling!

Then he started rolling backward!
"Help!" cried the butcher, as
the pancake rolled over him.

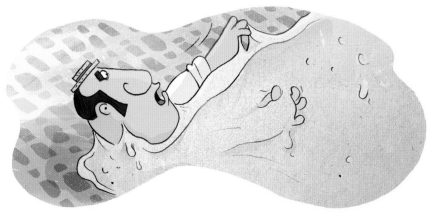

"Help!" cried the baker, as
he got stuck, too.

"Help!" cried the candlestick maker. "We're all stuck! And there's a GIANT coming!"

"Fee-fi-fo-fum!" cried the giant. "Dinnertime! My favorite! A giant pancake—or should I say MANcake? YUMMY!"

"Help!" cried the men.

"Help!" cried the pancake.

But then the pancake had an idea.

He rolled away from the giant.

"You're not fast enough!" squealed
the butcher as the giant gave chase.

"He'll catch us!" cried the baker. "Look out!" shouted the candlestick maker. "There's a RIVER!"
Sure enough, they rolled right into the water—SPLASH!

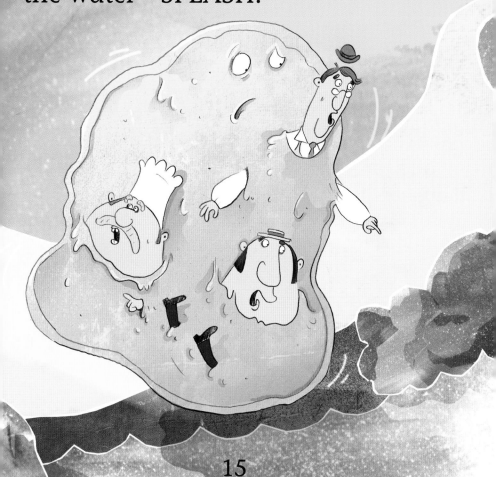

"We'll drown!" cried the butcher.

"I can't swim!" cried the baker.

"The giant's going to catch us!"
yelped the candlestick maker.

"Trust me," smiled the pancake.

The river was wide and the current was strong, but thanks to the pancake, they all floated safely on the water.

The giant tried to chase them
as they floated away, but he
was too slow.

Finally, they were swept to shore.

"We're safe!" cried the three men.

"Look, we're not stuck anymore!"

The water had softened the pancake's batter, and they all pulled themselves free. "You've saved us, Pancake!" they cheered.

But the pancake was now soggy and full of holes. He couldn't roll anymore.

"Go home," he told them.

"I'm glad you're safe."

Sadly, he watched them go.

But soon, the three of them
returned with a wheelbarrow
and frying pans!

Together, the townsfolk set to work repairing the pancake's holes, until finally he was even bigger than before.

27

The pancake jumped for joy and everyone cheered.

"Hip hip hooray for the biggest, brightest, very best pancake ever!"

Puzzle 1

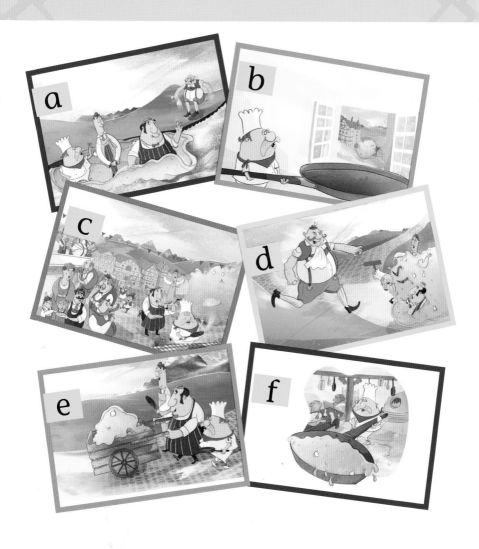

Put these pictures in the correct order. Which event do you think is the most important? Now try writing the story in your own words!

Puzzle 2

1. I love using frying pans.

2. I know how to float!

3. It's time for a tasty snack.

4. Fee-fi-fo- fum!

5. I am good at rolling!

6. My hat is very tall.

Choose the correct speech bubbles for each character. Can you think of any others? Turn the page to find the answers for both puzzles.

Notes for Adults

TADPOLES: Fairytale Twists are engaging, imaginative stories designed for early fluent readers. The books may also be used for read-alouds or shared reading with young children.

TADPOLES: Fairytale Twists are humorous stories with a unique twist on traditional fairy tales. Each story can be compared to the original fairy tale, or appreciated on its own. Fairy tales are a key type of literary text found in the Common Core State Standards.

The following PROMPTS before, during, and after reading support literacy skill development and can enrich shared reading experiences:

1. **Before Reading:** Do a picture walk through the book, previewing the illustrations. Ask the reader to predict what will happen in the story. For example, ask the reader what he or she thinks the twist in the story will be.

2. **During Reading:** Encourage the reader to use context clues and illustrations to determine the meaning of unknown words or phrases.

3. **During Reading:** Have the reader stop midway through the book to revisit his or her predictions. Does the reader wish to change his or her predictions based on what they have read so far?

4. **During and After Reading:** Encourage the reader to make different connections:
   Text-to-Text: How is this story similar to/ different from other stories you have read?
   Text-to-World: How are events in this story similar to/different from things that happen in the real world?
   Text-to-Self: Does a character or event in this story remind you of anything in your own life?

5. **After Reading:** Encourage the child to reread the story and to retell it using his or her own words. Invite the child to use the illustrations as a guide.

Here are other titles from TADPOLES: Fairytale Twists for you to enjoy:

Title	RLB	PB
Brownilocks and the Three Bowls of Cornflakes	978-0-7787-2459-9 RLB	978-0-7787-2511-4 PB
Cinderella's Big Foot	978-0-7787-0440-9 RLB	978-0-7787-0448-5 PB
Hansel and Gretel and the Green Witch	978-0-7787-1928-1 RLB	978-0-7787-1954-0 PB
Jack and the Bean Pie	978-0-7787-0441-6 RLB	978-0-7787-0449-2 PB
Little Bad Riding Hood	978-0-7787-0442-3 RLB	978-0-7787-0450-8 PB
Little Red Hen's Great Escape	978-0-7787-2461-3 RLB	978-0-7787-2512-1 PB
Princess Frog	978-0-7787-0443-0 RLB	978-0-7787-0452-2 PB
Rapunzel and the Prince of Pop	978-0-7787-1929-8 RLB	978-0-7787-1955-7 PB
Rumple Stilton Skin	978-0-7787-1930-4 RLB	978-0-7787-1956-4 PB
Sleeping Beauty—100 Years Later	978-0-7787-0444-7 RLB	978-0-7787-0479-9 PB
Snow White Sees the Light	978-0-7787-1931-1 RLB	978-0-7787-1957-1 PB
The Boy Who Cried Sheep!	978-0-7787-2471-1 RLB	978-0-7787-2567-1 PB
The Elves and the Trendy Shoes	978-0-7787-1932-8 RLB	978-0-7787-1958-8 PB
The Emperor's New Uniform	978-0-7787-1933-5 RLB	978-0-7787-1959-5 PB
The Lovely Duckling	978-0-7787-0445-4 RLB	978-0-7787-0480-5 PB
The Ninjabread Man	978-0-7787-2472-8 RLB	978-0-7787-2568-8 PB
The Pied Piper and the Wrong Song	978-0-7787-1934-2 RLB	978-0-7787-1960-1 PB
The Princess and the Frozen Peas	978-0-7787-0446-1 RLB	978-0-7787-0481-2 PB
The Three Frilly Goats Fluff	978-0-7787-1935-9 RLB	978-0-7787-1961-8 PB
The Three Little Pigs and the New Neighbor	978-0-7787-0447-8 RLB	978-0-7787-0482-9 PB
Thumbelina Thinks Big!	978-0-7787-2473-5 RLB	978-0-7787-2569-5 PB

Answers

Puzzle 1
The correct order is: 1f, 2b, 3d, 4a, 5e, 6c

Puzzle 2
The baker: 1, 6
The pancake: 2, 5
The giant: 3, 4